The House on the Volcano

(Original title: Kimo and Madame Pele)

by VIRGINIA NIELSEN

Illustrated by Ursula Koering

SCHOLASTIC BOOK SERVICES
NEW YORK • TORONTO • LONDON • AUCKLAND • SYDNEY

The author wishes to acknowledge her indebtedness to the Hawaii Natural History Association and to the Hawaiian Volcano Observatory, especially to Dr. Howard A. Powers, who was kind enough to read this account of an imaginary eruption on the volcano-scarred Puna coast of Hawaii.

 This edition is published by Scholastic Book Services, a division of Scholastic Magazines, Inc., by arrangement with David McKay Company, Inc., who first published the book under the title of KIMO AND MADAME PELE.

1st printing . . . . March 1970

Printed in the U.S.A.

To My Mother

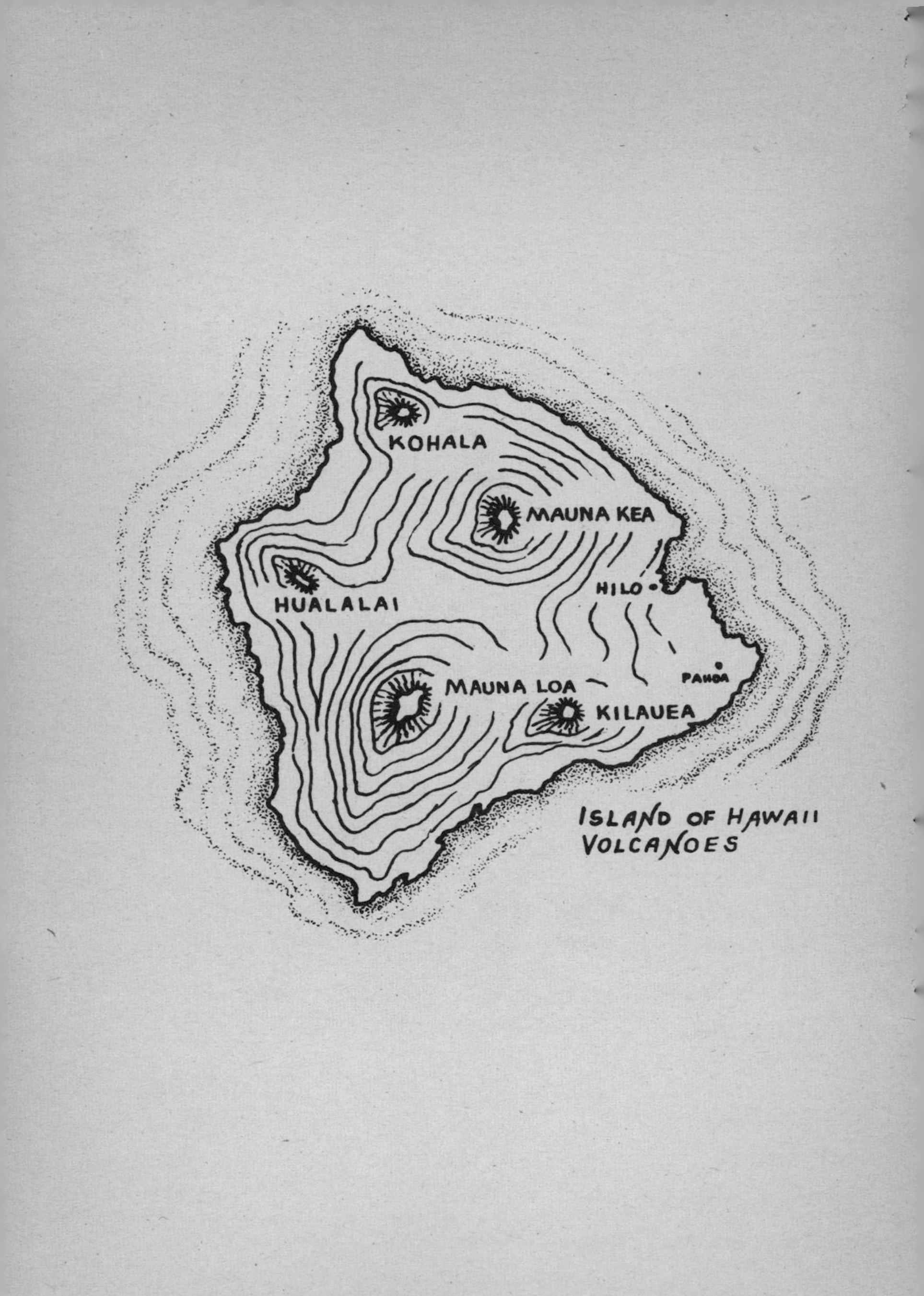
KOHALA
MAUNA KEA
HUALALAI
HILO
MAUNA LOA
PAHOA
KILAUEA
ISLAND OF HAWAII
VOLCANOES

1

KIMO LIVED with his grandmother on the side of a volcano. Their house sat at the edge of an old lava flow on the east coast of the island of Hawaii. An orchard of papaya trees stood at its back, and a lawn lay between the house and the black cinder road.

On clear days, if he climbed the dark ridge of lava, Kimo could see the crater rim of the volcano Kilauea (Kee lu-*way*-a). Twice since Kimo was born the volcano had erupted fountains of fiery lava.

At night when he lay in his bed, Kimo could hear the crash of the surf against the black sand beach less than a mile away, where the lava had once flowed to the sea.

One morning Kimo was wakened very early by the barking of his dog and the noisy rattle of his windows, shaking in their frames. When he realized his bed was shaking too, his heart began to beat very fast. He called loudly, "Tutu?"

From the room where his grandmother slept came her deep warm chuckle and comforting voice. "Don't be afraid, Kimo. It is only Madame Pele turning over in her sleep."

Madame Pele was Tutu's friend who lived in Kilauea Crater. Some called her the goddess of fire and some said Pele was the spirit of the volcano, but Tutu always spoke of her as "my friend, Madame Pele."

While his bed shivered and his windows rattled, sometimes as loud and fast as the chatter of the mynah birds in the coco palms, Kimo remembered the stories his grandmother had told him about her friend.

Madame Pele did not always stay in the crater that was her home. Sometimes she appeared to Tutu in the clouds blown gently across the sky by the trade winds. At other times she took the shape of a beautiful young girl dressed in red, or a very old woman in rags. Kimo had never seen Madame Pele, but he hoped someday he would.

Presently his grandmother arose. Kimo heard her in the kitchen, filling her coffee pot and slicing one of the papayas he had picked for her last night.

He got up and washed the sleep out of his eyes and put on his pants and his clean shirt. It was yellow, with a pattern of white plumeria blossoms.

In the kitchen he sat down before the golden wedge of papaya and the tall glass of milk his grandmother had set out for him. "Tell me about Madame Pele," he begged.

Tutu laughed and sat across the table from him with her cup of coffee. Her great body spread itself comfortably over her chair, draped in folds of her brilliant red-and-white *muumuu* (long, loose dress).

One reason Kimo loved his grandmother so much was that she was never in such a hurry she couldn't tell him stories. And when the school bus honked for him, she often said, "Eat your breakfast. The bus will wait." Stepping to the door, she would call across the lawn to the bus driver, "*Aloha,* Pete! How is your *keiki* (boy) this morning?"

Then Pete would idle his motor and brag about his little boy while Kimo finished his cereal.

This morning Tutu told Kimo the story of her grandfather. "Many years ago," she began, "my grandfather was travelling on horseback from his farm to a village on the Kona coast. The trail went over an ancient lava flow and it was very rough. He passed an old woman, all bent over and dragging a heavy sack.

"He stopped his horse and said, 'Old woman, you must be tired. Climb up behind me.'

"She didn't speak. She just handed him her sack

and climbed up. He thought she was pretty spry for an old one. He handed back her sack and started his horse."

Now came the part Kimo liked. He shook some cornflakes from the box into a bowl and poured what was left of his milk over it, then settled down to listen while he ate.

"Grandfather said to himself, 'That poor old one is nothing but skin and bones. My horse does not even feel her weight.' He said, 'Hold on, old woman, or you will fall.'

"There was no answer. My grandfather turned his head. *There was no old woman there!*"

"*Ai!*" exclaimed Kimo, with an excited laugh.

"Two days later the volcano erupted and a river of fiery rocks ran down to the sea. But when the river of fire reached my grandfather's farm, it split in two and came together again after it had spared his fields.

"And that was how my grandfather knew the old woman he had befriended was Madame Pele."

Just as Tutu finished her story, the little house rocked again. The milk sloshed out of Kimo's bowl, and a knife skittered off the drainboard to the floor.

Tutu bent down to pick it up. "Never be rude to a strange woman," she warned Kimo. "She may be Madame Pele in disguise."

The bus honked. Tutu laughed at Kimo as he hurriedly spooned up the last cornflake, snatched his books, and ran for the door. She followed him to the porch and waved to the driver as Kimo dashed down the long front yard to the gate, his dog racing beside him.

"Stay, Poki!" Kimo ordered, as he scrambled aboard.

There was a vacant seat beside Tokiko, who lived on the farm next to his. He knew she had saved it for him, but he was not going to sit beside a girl with the whole bus looking on. He slipped into a seat just behind her. Too late, he saw he was sitting beside his worst enemy, Hiroshi.

He half stood up again, but when he saw Hiroshi start to grin, he twisted around and pretended he had risen to look back at his dog. Poki was sitting by the road, gazing after the bus with her tongue hanging out and her tail scraping back and forth across the black cinders as she tried to wag it.

"Old dumb dog," Kimo complained. "She's too lazy to stand up and wag her tail, but she barks every time there's an earthquake."

Tokiko squirmed around in her seat. "She must have barked all last night then."

"You know what that quaking means?" Hiroshi

said, in his superior way. "It means the volcano is going to erupt."

"Who says so?" Kimo challenged. Hiroshi always thought he knew everything. The trouble was, he did know a great deal. Kimo would not have minded so much if Hiroshi were not always so eager to tell what he knew. It could be very annoying.

"Want to bet?" Hiroshi asked, his black eyes snapping and alive under his brush-cut black hair. When he was excited, even his ears seemed to stand out at attention. "I'll bet anything Kilauea erupts within three days!"

"Nobody knows when Kilauea will erupt," Kimo scoffed.

"The volcanologists do!"

Tokiko turned around again to stare at him. "What's *that?*"

"A volcanologist is a scientist who studies volcanoes."

"Then why didn't you say so?" Kimo demanded scornfully.

"I did!"

"Quiet, back there!" the bus driver yelled.

Hiroshi lowered his voice and had the last word. "That's what I'm going to be some day," he boasted. "A volcanologist."

Kimo raised his eyebrows at Tokiko, but to his

disgust she was looking admiringly at Hiroshi. Girls! he thought.

The bus was taking them past small fields of bananas and sugar cane and dark-leafed lichee trees, stopping now and then to pick up more passengers. When it reached the village, Kimo noticed there were many men and women on the streets. They were gathered in knots here and there, talking.

The bus pulled up in the schoolyard, and marching out of it with the other pupils, Kimo noticed something else very strange. As he walked toward the school building, the solid ground felt as if it were heaving up and sinking away like small waves under his surfboard.

It was a queer feeling.

2

MISS PRINCE WAS in her room, writing some spelling words on the board with coloured chalk. A fresh hibiscus blossom was lying on her desk.

Kimo liked the way Miss Prince brought fresh colours into her room. Even her hair brightened the day. It was a warm golden red that reminded Kimo of a ripe mango. Secretly, he thought his teacher must be the most beautiful *haole* — Tutu's word for light-skinned persons — in the world. She had come to Hawaii from California.

The words she was writing were: "volcano," "eruption," "crater," "crust," "lava," and "magma." "Eruption" and "magma" were in red. When she wrote the final word, "volcanologist," Hiroshi turned and gave Kimo a superior look.

The room was noisy this morning. The girls were chattering nervously about what had happened at home.

"Our lamp fell over!"

"Some dishes fell out of our cupboard!"

Miss Prince laid down her chalk and turned around to smile at them. "Good morning, children." She looked around the room, and her gaze stopped on a girl in the fifth row. "Lani, will you lead us in the Pledge of Allegiance?"

Just as they began, another tremor shook the school building. It was so violent that books slid off the desk, and the chalk bounced out of the groove under the chalkboard. Miss Prince was caught off balance. She teetered backward on her high heels and braced herself against the chalkboard wall.

Hiroshi began chanting, "Earthquake! Earthquake!" as if he were the only one who knew what was happening. Some of the boys joined in his chant. The girls were squealing and one began to cry.

"Dear me!" Miss Prince said then, in such a small voice that the room quieted instantly. "That was a very sharp tremor!"

"Were you scared, Miss Prince?" Lani asked.

"Pick up your books, children," she replied, although they were already picking them up. Then she smiled, and Kimo felt himself relax. "Yes, Lani, it did startle me."

The girls began chattering again while the lunch money was being counted. Miss Prince raised her voice. "I think we should talk about earthquakes this morning, but one at a time, please! Can anyone tell us why we have earthquakes?"

Hiroshi shouted, "Because we live on a volcano!"

"My, we're excited this morning," Miss Prince said. "We usually wait until we're called on."

Kimo, who was already waving his hand, shot a triumphant look at Hiroshi as Miss Prince said, "Yes, Kimo?"

"Madame Pele, whose land this is, is turning over in her sleep." He heard Hiroshi snort, but he went right on. "If she is angry when she wakes up, she will toss hot rocks into the air."

Out of the corner of his eye he saw Hiroshi waving his hand wildly. "Her home is in Kilauea," Kimo went on, more loudly, "but sometimes she walks across the land. When she stamps her foot, lava bursts out of the ground. But if you are her friend, the lava will not destroy you."

"Thank you, Kimo," Miss Prince said, looking doubtful. "Hiroshi?"

Kimo's worst enemy stood up. "The Hawaiian Islands are all volcanic craters," he said importantly. "The crater we live on is still active. That means about twenty miles down, under the earth's crust, there's a layer of magma, which is melted rock and gases, and there's pressure on it from the weight of all the mountains and everything on top of it — "

Kimo listened in angry disbelief, as Hiroshi talked so fast and so eagerly that his words were tripping over one another. He sounded as if he were reading from a book.

"— so the lava's always looking for a weak place in the earth's crust and when it finds it, the gases start expanding, and the lava comes up faster and faster, and the earth shakes — and that's how the volcanologists can tell there's going to be an eruption, by measuring the earthquakes!"

Kimo could stand it no longer. "My grandmother has seen Pele!" he shouted.

"So has my father!" a boy behind him spoke up. "He passed her on the Saddle Road only last week. When he went back to see what an old woman was doing out alone at midnight, he couldn't find her."

"He was seeing things!" Hiroshi snorted.

"She's real!" a girl cried. "My mother says she always shows herself before an eruption. My mother says — "

"Superstition!" Hiroshi exclaimed interrupting her, and then everyone began trying to talk at once.

"That's enough, children!" Miss Prince's face was getting quite red. She turned and added another word to the list on the board. "Kimo, can you tell us what a 'legend' is?"

Kimo got slowly to his feet, "My dog Poki got

her name from a legend." It was one of Tutu's stories. She had heard it from the old ones. "In the old days people believed there was a great spotted dog who travelled at night. There was something magic about him because only the ones he loved could see him. Lots of spotted dogs are named after him."

"Do you see any similarity between Poki's story and the one you told us about Madame Pele?" Miss Prince asked gently. "Pele is not seen by everyone either. She is magic too. She can change her form and when she stamps her foot, lava flows out of the ground."

"Many persons have seen Pele," Kimo said stubbornly.

"The old Hawaiians were not scientists. Perhaps they explained the eruptions of their volcanoes with stories about a goddess of fire because they did not have a scientific explanation."

Kimo gazed at his teacher in dismay. She was saying Tutu's friend was only a legend. She was on Hiroshi's side!

"Today, at the Observatory at Kilauea Crater, scientists are collecting information from which we can learn more and more about volcanoes. *Volcanologists* study each *eruption* — " Miss Prince pointed lightly to each word as she pronounced it — "when *magma,* which is liquid *lava,* rises through the earth's *crust* and flows out of the *crater* of the *volcano.*"

"What makes it decide to rise?" Kimo persisted doggedly.

Miss Prince flushed slightly. Instead of answering, she asked, "How many of you have visited the Observatory at Hawaii National Park?"

Only Hiroshi and a few others put up their hands.

"Perhaps some day we can make a class trip to the Observatory and see for ourselves what they are doing there. In the meantime, I will talk to a friend of mine who works there and ask him to tell me more about it so I can answer your questions."

She turned her back on them and erased the words from the board. "Will the monitor please pass the paper?"

Some of the pupils groaned. Kimo sat down, but he did not pick up his pencil. "All the same," he said, loudly, "you should never be rude to a strange woman."

Miss Prince looked a little startled. "Why do you say that, Kimo?"

There was a titter somewhere in the room, but he paid no attention. He looked at Miss Prince, and she did not look away.

"I'll remember that, Kimo," she said, at last. "Are you ready, class?" And she began the spelling test.

3

KIMO AND HIROSHI always played on opposite sides at volley ball during recess. Kimo was reaching for a high one when Hiroshi yelled, "Hey, Kimo! Look! There's Madame Pele!"

Kimo missed the ball.

He knew he was being mocked, but he had not been able to keep himself from looking where Hiroshi pointed. Then his heart leaped, and he forgot to run after the ball. A bent old woman in a faded *muumuu* and a wide straw hat that hid her face was walking painfully along the road, carrying a full shopping bag.

"Madame Pele! Madame Pele!" The shouts rose all over the playground. Some were from Kimo's friends who sounded as if they really believed the old woman to be Pele, but others were from friends of Hiroshi who were mocking Kimo.

The old woman heard the shouts. She stopped and stared at them.

All at once a small whirlwind came flying out of a group of girls. Tokiko's fists were doubled up, and her eyes were hot with anger.

"You hush!" she told Hiroshi. "That's my grandmother. She's carrying her eggs to the store."

Kimo looked again. It was, indeed, the *tutu* of Tokiko, who lived in her own little house in the village.

Hiroshi laughed. "Kimo thinks she's Pele."

Right then Kimo decided he had had enough of Hiroshi's grinning face. He elbowed Tokiko aside and, lowering his head, ran straight at the other boy as hard as he could.

He saw Hiroshi's fists come up and then he saw Hiroshi's feet step aside. He knew if he raised his head he would get a blow right on the jaw, so he put out his foot and tripped his tormentor and fell on him.

They rolled over and over in the pink dust of the playground. But almost at once Mr. Hoopai, the principal, was there, reaching down to pull them apart.

"Kimo! Hiroshi! I'll see you two in my office," he said sternly.

"Yes, sir," they mumbled, both breathing hard. Hiroshi's face was smudged with dirt, and Kimo's elbow was bleeding where he had scraped it on the hard ground.

Still holding each of them by an arm, the principal marched them toward the school building. When he noticed the blood trickling down Kimo's arm, he said, "Hiroshi, you wait for me in my office. Kimo, you come with me."

He led Kimo down the hall to the school nurse's room. Mrs. Oana looked up from her desk, her broad Hawaiian face smiling and calm. "What have we here?"

"Nothing serious," Mr. Hoopai told her. "Just a little skin scraped off. He is to report to my office as soon as you finish with him. Understand, Kimo?"

"Yes, sir."

The principal left. Mrs. Oana stood up, her white skirts rustling as she crossed to her medicine cabinet. She moistened some cotton with something that smelled pleasantly strong and began to swab the blood and grime from Kimo's elbow with gentle strokes.

"What happened, Kimo? You were fighting?"

He nodded.

"What about?"

"Madame Pele."

Mrs. Oana stopped stroking the skinned place on his elbow and looked at him. "Madame Pele," she repeated in a strange voice. "Why were you fighting about her?"

"Hiroshi doesn't think there is any Madame Pele."

Mrs. Oana bent her head over his arm and finished cleaning it. She picked up a bandage and tore off its plastic envelope. "And what do you think, Kimo?"

"Tutu has seen her." He watched as she crisscrossed the bandage with tape to hold it in place. "But Miss Prince says she is a legend."

"What does a *haole* know about it?" Mrs. Oana asked softly in Hawaiian.

Kimo looked up in surprise. Perhaps she did not know he would understand, for she had spoken as if to herself. But his grandmother was one of the old women who still sometimes used the ancient language.

"Mrs. Oana, do you believe Madame Pele is real?"

For a moment the school nurse did not say anything. Then she replied, in a low but firm voice, "Kimo, I *know* Madame Pele is real."

He felt a prickle of excitement run up his back. "How do you know?" he demanded.

She sat back in her chair. Her beautiful brown eyes had a soft glow. "Last year when I went to Honolulu, I visited a lovely park. I had colour film in my camera and I was taking pictures. A young girl who was wearing a red dress stood under a very old breadfruit tree watching me."

Kimo shivered. Red was Pele's colour.

The nurse went on. "I thought, How pretty she is, standing under that magnificent tree! I asked if I might take her picture. She smiled and nodded, and I snapped it.

"But when I had the roll of film developed," Mrs. Oana continued, in a lower tone, "I found I had a nice snapshot of the old breadfruit tree, *but the girl in the red dress had disappeared!* I knew then it had been Madame Pele in disguise."

Kimo's heart was pounding with excitement. Wait until I tell them! he thought. Miss Prince — Hiroshi — the whole class! They would have to believe him now.

But first he had to go to the principal's office and be scolded for fighting in the playing yard.

"*Mahalo,* thank you, Mrs. Oana!" he cried and ran out of her room and down the hall.

The scolding was not as bad as he feared. For one thing, the school building shook with a sharp tremor just as he entered the principal's office and continued to tremble and rattle the windows while he and Hiroshi stood beside Mr. Hoopai's desk.

Mr. Hoopai did not seem to have his mind on scolding them. As he talked, he repeatedly turned his eyes toward the rattling windows. When he looked in their direction, he seemed to be looking right through them.

Then the bell rang, and he said, "You may walk, not run, to your class without speaking to each other. Is that understood?"

"Yes, sir," Kimo said, eyes straight ahead, and heard Hiroshi parroting him.

But out in the hall he glared at his enemy and dragged his finger across his throat.

Hiroshi only drew one side of his mouth down in the superior smile that Kimo found so irritating, as if he were a quarrelsome younger brother who was not very smart.

4

When they reached the classroom, they found Miss Prince had a visitor, a thin, sunburned young man dressed in khaki with a pair of binoculars hanging around his neck. Miss Prince looked slightly flustered and very pretty.

"Boys and girls," she said, as Kimo and Hiroshi slid into their seats, "this is Dr. Gerard, of the Volcano Observatory. He has something important to tell us, and afterward he has promised to give us a few minutes of his time in which you may ask questions."

Dr. Gerard had thick yellow hair and a shy smile. "I volunteered to bring you some information sheets prepared by Civil Defense authorities. Miss Prince will pass them out, and we ask that you take them home to your parents. It is important that your parents receive this information, for it tells what help will be available if the volcano erupts."

Miss Prince quietly handed the mimeographed sheets to the first row to be passed along. Tokiko raised her hand timidly and asked, "Is Kilauea going to erupt again?"

"We think so, yes."

"When?" several eager voices asked.

"No one can answer that," the volcanologist said with a quick smile.

Ha! Kimo thought, and flashed a look of scorn at Hiroshi.

"We think it will be soon and we think we know that it is most likely to occur along the rift where it has erupted before."

"How do you know?" Kimo demanded. He had felt an instant liking for the shy man standing before them in his work clothes, but he tried to deny it. After all, the scientist was on Hiroshi's side.

"That's a long story. It involves many years of collecting evidence and interpreting information about volcanoes." He looked around at the board. Miss Prince offered him a piece of chalk, which he took with a smile of thanks that pinked the teacher's cheeks.

Kimo watched closely as he drew a volcanic crater and labelled it "Kilauea." Then he drew a chimneylike opening extending from the crater down through the earth's crust. He saw Miss Prince's red chalk and with it drew a lake of hot lava below the earth's crust, with a red finger pushing upward.

"Around the crater we have instruments called tiltmeters that tell us when lava is rising to the surface. We have found that the volcano swells like a balloon before an eruption, making its sides tilt outward. After an eruption, the swelling goes down again. For the past month Kilauea has been swelling."

As he talked, the school began shaking again. The room grew very quiet, except for the volcanologist's calm voice and the rattle, rattle of the windows in their frames.

Dr. Gerard turned back to the chalkboard. He made a series of short, sharp strokes filling up the chimney of the volcano. Then he drew a sloping line running away from Kilauea's crater. He labelled it "rift zone."

"When the lava cools after a volcanic eruption, it becomes basalt, a hard rock that sometimes plugs up the chimney or throat of the volcano. Before it can erupt again it must crack and shatter this plug. If it cannot, it will find a weaker path running out through faults in the flank of the volcano.

"When we know there is an area of cracked and faulted rock, we call it a 'rift zone.' Hot magma entering a crack exerts pressure. The crack widens and the rocks move a little, causing the kind of shallow earthquake that we have learned means lava is flowing beneath the earth's surface.

"At the Volcano Observatory and at other places around the island, we have instruments called seismographs to measure and record these earth tremors. From them we can learn the direction in which the lava is moving underground.

"The swarms of earth tremors you have been having for the past two weeks indicate that the eruption we believe is coming may be centered in your village, which lies along a rift."

He paused, and a small voice in the back of the room asked, "Will some of us die?"

Dr. Gerard caught himself in the middle of a startled laugh. "No," he said gently. "No lives have been lost in a volcanic eruption in Hawaii in a very long time. We keep such a close watch on our volcanoes at the Observatory that we are able to warn you in advance and make provisions for your safety, as we are doing now."

He smiled. "Hawaii is the only place in the world where it is safe to baby-sit a volcano — which is what we are doing at the Observatory."

There was relieved laughter in the room.

"If it is necessary to leave your homes," he finished, "National Guard and plantation trucks will be sent to help move you and your animals to a safe place. Tell your parents to keep your radios on for announcements from Civil Defense authorities."

Miss Prince said, "Thank you very much, Dr. Gerard."

Hiroshi was waving his hand importantly. "Dr. Gerard, what makes the lava start to rise?"

"Probably expanding gases within the lava. We are still collecting evidence."

"What kind of evidence?"

"Well, for example, during an eruption our geochemists collect samples of gas and magma for analysis in the laboratory. The mystery of what lies at the centre of our earth is as great as that which lies out in space — and for some of us it is even more fascinating."

Hiroshi's eyes glowed.

Kimo was both angered and confused. Not once had Dr. Gerard mentioned Madame Pele. Recklessly, he spoke up. "I guess Madame Pele is waking up, all right!"

Dr. Gerard retorted, "We don't think she ever sleeps!"

The class laughed appreciatively, and Kimo shot a look of triumph at Hiroshi. While Miss Prince thanked Dr. Gerard again for giving them his valuable time, Kimo had a brilliant idea. The scientist had admitted they did not know everything about the volcano. They were still collecting evidence. Well, he would collect evidence too!

All afternoon he thought about it. Tutu's grandfather had given a ride on his horse to an old woman who disappeared in broad daylight, just two days before the volcano erupted. Surely that was evidence?

Mrs. Oana had taken a picture of a beautiful girl dressed in Pele's colour, but the camera had looked right through her! Surely, there must be other evidence that Madame Pele existed. He would collect so much evidence that no one could deny it!

When he arrived home, Tutu was on the porch grating coconut for *haupia,* the white pudding that was Kimo's favorite dessert. He put the sheet of paper in her ample lap.

"What's this?" she asked carelessly, not bothering to read it.

"The man from the Observatory gave it to us. He says there is going to be an eruption."

Tutu handed him a chunk of brown-skinned coconut. "I could have told him that."

"It says if they evacuate the village, they will take everybody to Pahoa school."

"No need for us to go anywhere," she said comfortably.

Kimo munched the fresh coconut. "Tutu, if you wanted to see Madame Pele, where would you go?"

She looked at him and laughed. "If I wanted to see Madame Pele!" she mocked. "Madame Pele chooses the time to show herself. She doesn't show herself to everyone, you know."

"Do you think she would show herself to me?"

"Have you ever made an offering of the red *lehua* blossom? Do you offer her the first *ohelo* berries before you eat her sacred fruit?"

Kimo shook his head, abashed by the good-natured scorn in his grandmother's tone.

"Then be glad she hasn't shown herself to you!"

"But where have you seen her, Tutu?"

She gazed off across the trees at the green cane climbing the mountain slopes. "Once I saw her in the fire when the men were burning off the cane. Once I saw her face in the clouds and heard her speak in the lightning. Twice I saw her at the warm springs."

"Pele's bathtub!" Kimo breathed. Why had he not thought of that? He edged off the porch and whistled Poki up from her snoozing.

"Where you go now, Kimo?" his grandmother called after him, but he pretended he did not hear her.

5

KIMO STARTED through the papaya trees as if he were going to take a short path to Tokiko's house, but when he came out of the orchard, he turned and began climbing the old lava flow.

It was rough going. The larger chunks of lava had not yet been broken down by the rain and the wind into black earth, and the ground between them was covered with low-growing shrubs and stunted *ohia* trees, always the first to take root in thc cracks in new lava.

Kimo kept a sharp watch for a spot of red in the grey-green leaves. The *ohia* would not feather out in the *lehua* blossoms Pele loved until spring, but on the low-growing *ohelo* he might still find a branch of the drying berries for the goddess if the birds had not eaten them all!

Poki was finding it easier climbing. Sometimes she ran far ahead of him, then pretended to be very busy sniffing round a bush until he caught up with her. She would keep sniffing and sniffing until he passed and left her behind, then she would give a joyous bark and come leaping up to him again.

When Kimo reached the spine of the lava flow, he paused to catch his breath and look around him. He could see the tin roof of his grandmother's house, silvery in the afternoon light. Not far away, almost lost in the leaves of banana, papaya, and shade trees, was the dark green house where Tokiko lived. Beyond it was the sea.

A narrow paved road followed the coast, disappearing behind the black promontory of lava, then reappearing to follow the sea for a space before it turned inland into the forest around the warm springs.

Through the trees thin wisps of steam drifted up from the pool, hidden under its green umbrella of leaves. Kimo started down the slope toward it.

As he scrambled over one rocky patch, he had the uncomfortable sensation that the rocks under his feet were warmer than they should be. It reminded him of what Dr. Gerard had said about hot lava moving beneath the earth's surface. He shivered and tried to put the picture out of his mind.

"What does a *haole* know about it?" he said

loudly. Behind him, Poki let out a growl. He turned. "What is it, Poki?"

Barking, she dashed past him, leaping over rocks and low bushes as she hurried down toward the trees that hid the springs. "Here, Poki! Here, Poki!" Kimo shouted in vain. His dog paid no attention. Far below him she stopped, barking furiously.

Kimo strained to see what Poki had spied. When he found it, his breath almost stopped in his throat. Far down the ridge, near the coast, was a tiny figure in red. It seemed to linger for a moment on the edge of the forest that hid the springs. Then it disappeared.

At the same time, Poki dashed into the trees. An instant later her frantic barking abruptly ended. A chill ran up Kimo's back. What had happened to make Poki stop barking so suddenly?

He was not sure he wanted to see Madame Pele, after all, but the thought of what might be happening to his dog sent him scrambling down the lava and plunging into the trees.

Far ahead he glimpsed a flash of red. "Poki!" he shouted.

Poki barked once.

Kimo ran on. At last he burst through the trees into the cleared picnic area around the still warm pool. Kneeling beside the water, idly stirring it with a branch, was Tokiko. Her dusty bare toes peeped from beneath the hem of her red *muumuu.*

Beside Tokiko, Poki was sitting on her tail and trying to wag it, in her silly way.

"It was you!" Kimo gasped, out of breath. He was so relieved to find Poki all in one piece and so disappointed that Tokiko was not Madame Pele that he felt almost angry. "What are you doing here, anyway?"

"I have as much right here as you have!" Tokiko flashed, tossing her straight black hair.

"Hello, Kimo!" Mrs. Yamasaki called. "Can you stay and eat with Tokiko?"

For the first time Kimo saw the thermos and packages of food on the picnic table Tokiko's mother was setting on the other side of the pool. Her father was broiling *teriyaki* steaks on a charcoal *hibachi* at the other end of the table, and her younger brother and sister were walking around the pool toward their parents.

Kimo began backing away. Not much use waiting around here for Madame Pele! "No, ma'am," he called, politely. "I just came down to see if Poki was in trouble."

Tokiko looked interested. "What kind of trouble?" she asked, but Kimo did not intend to tell her he had taken her for Madame Pele!

"Oh, she gets too snoopy," he said carelessly.

"Good old Poki," Tokiko crooned, putting her arm around the dog's neck. "Don't you want to stay and eat with us, Kimo?"

"I've got other things to do." He regretted his hasty words at once, for Tokiko looked at him very curiously. He turned his back before she could ask him more questions and, whistling Poki to heel, started back the long way, by the coast road.

As he walked, he watched the moving clouds and tried to see the figure of a woman in their ever-changing shapes. But the goddess was still hiding her face from him.

6

THAT NIGHT the earthquakes were so sharp and so frequent that Kimo could not sleep. He kept dozing off, then waking up with the sound of his heart beating hard in his ears, and the noisy rattle of his windows filling his room.

Outside Poki began howling, and Tutu called irritably, "Kimo, shut that dog up!"

Kimo got out of bed and padded to the back door. As soon as he opened the screen, Poki came in, not in a joyous bound as she usually did, but wriggling across the floor on her stomach and licking Kimo's bare toes in ecstatic relief.

"Shhh," he cautioned her and led the way back to his room. In vain he tried to get Poki to lie down on the floor beside the bed. She insisted on leaping on the bed and stretching out on her stomach with her nose on her paws, as close as she could get to Kimo's face.

He dozed off again but was wakened by a scratching and a mewing at his window. It was Fluff, the cat, who was trying to get in this time.

Kimo sat up in bed and reached over to unlatch the window screen and hold it out while Fluff crawled in. Then the three of them settled down to try to sleep.

He could not tell how long he slept, because there were clouds across the moon, but when he wakened the next time his bed was jerking, Poki was whining, and Fluff set her claws into him right through his pajamas.

Kimo had had enough! He jumped out of bed and ran into his grandmother's room. There was a heavy thump as Poki jumped off the bed to follow him, then a lighter thump as Fluff followed Poki.

All three of them hopped into bed with Tutu and, strangely, she did not grumble as she made room.

"Are you asleep, Tutu?" Kimo asked some time later.

The bed shook, and Kimo did not know whether it was from a small tremor or his grandmother's amiable snort as she replied, "Who could sleep?"

Poki wriggled as if she were trying to snuggle deeper into the mattress, and Fluff, who had taken half of Kimo's pillow, stretched her neck until her cool nose touched his cheek. That was the way they spent the rest of the night, while the house rattled and shook around them.

When it was light, Kimo got up and prepared to go to school as usual. While he and his grandmother were having breakfast, Hanalei, who lived on the other side of Tutu's banana patch, appeared silently at the back door. "My father says if you want to go to Pahoa, he will take you with us."

"What for I want to go to Pahoa?" Tutu inquired.

"Because the lava is coming."

"I haven't seen any lava."

"My father says it is coming."

"Tell your father we're not afraid of the lava." There was a shade of scorn in Tutu's voice. After Hanalei had disappeared, his bare feet going as silently as they had come, she said darkly, "That man's got sins to answer for! No wonder he's afraid of Madame Pele."

Kimo said nothing, but he knew what she was talking about. Hanalei's father's sin had been letting his chickens stray over into Tutu's vegetable garden.

When she rose to refill her coffee cup, she switched on the radio on the shelf above her sink. Kimo listened as the announcer told them earth tremors, centered in the village, were almost continuous and the Observatory scientists, who were watching developments closely, said that could mean lava was moving toward the surface.

A few minutes later, the school bus pulled up and honked for Kimo as usual.

Tokiko was not on the bus this morning. The bus was almost empty. But Hiroshi was there, dispensing information in his usual irritating way. This morning he was full of chatter about seismographs and "swarms" of earth tremors and crystallized lava lakes and what he was going to have to study to get a job on a volcano.

"When I graduate from college, I'm going to get a job as a scientific aide," he told everyone within range of his voice. "I'll have to take lots of mathematics and physics and chemistry. Then I'm going to save my money and go back to school and specialize. I'm going to specialize in volcanoes!" His eyes glowed, and he jiggled with excitement.

"I'm collecting evidence," Kimo said significantly, and would not explain what he meant even though Hiroshi pressed him.

When Miss Prince called the roll, only half the class was present. Kimo could not keep his mind on his classwork. Miss Prince herself seemed absent-minded. She had left the door of the classroom open and frequently she glanced into the hall.

There was expectancy in the room and a strange excitement pulling at them from outside it. The principal walked by their open door several times, once with Dr. Gerard, who looked as if he had not changed his clothes since yesterday.

A little before the morning recess, Miss Prince apparently received a signal from someone in the hall. She stopped in the middle of a sentence and said, "Children, the village is being evacuated as a safety measure." She raised her voice in order to be heard over the noisy rattle of the windows. "We have been asked to dismiss school and return you to your homes so that you can be evacuated with your parents."

Kimo put up his hand. "What if we don't live in the village?"

His teacher looked distracted. "Tell your grandmother to keep her radio on, Kimo."

The class stood and marched, two by two, out of the school and into the waiting busses. Kimo's bus went through the village. Along the streets it passed, many people were loading their belongings into trucks and cars, preparing to leave their homes and their stores.

Halfway down Kamehameha Street, the bus stopped, and the driver opened his door and jumped out. Kimo stuck his head through the window to see why they were stopped.

A barrier had been erected across the street. Several men were standing in front of it, looking at something. When the bus driver walked toward them they moved, and Kimo saw that there was a great crack across the street.

Hiroshi had his head out of the next window. "It's a graben," he cried excitedly.

"A *what?*" In spite of his annoyance, Kimo could not keep the question back.

"A graben. That means the earth has cracked open

along a fault in the rocks." Hiroshi's eyes were wide. "Maybe the lava will come up there!"

A patrol car pulled up alongside the bus right under Kimo. Tutu's friend, Dan Mookini, was driving it. He opened the door and got out, looking tall and impressive in his police officer's uniform with its shiny badge.

"Hey, Dan! *Aloha!*" Kimo cried.

The big man turned. When he saw Kimo, he smiled and came over to the bus. "*Aloha,* Kimo! Has your *tutu* left her house yet?"

"She says we don't have to leave."

Big Dan's smile went away. "Why not, Kimo?"

"Because Madame Pele is her friend."

Big Dan took off his officer's cap and brushed his curling black hair with his hand. "Well, now, Pele is not a very dependable friend, you know."

Kimo sneaked a glance at Hiroshi to see if his worst enemy had noticed that the policeman did not laugh at Madame Pele.

"Is she really a goddess?" he asked Big Dan.

But just then the bus driver, who had jumped back into his seat, raced his big motor, drowning Kimo's question, and put the bus in reverse.

Big Dan called something as they backed away, but Kimo could not hear what it was.

7

ALL THAT AFTERNOON cars and pickup trucks passed on the road in front of Kimo's house, loaded with the possessions of families who were fleeing Pele's wrath. Tutu went about her work as usual, waving good-naturedly at friends, but refusing all offers to join them.

Just before supper, Poki began barking a noisy alarm. Kimo ran to the door. A strange car had turned in their drive. It came slowly up to the house and stopped behind Tutu's ancient automobile.

"*Aloha!*" called the man from his car.

Kimo went out on the porch and ordered Poki back. From the doorway, Tutu answered, "*Aloha!*"

The stranger got out of his car and came up to the porch. "I'm from Civil Defense, Tutu," he said, wiping sweat from his face with a white handkerchief. "I came to see if you need transportation to Pahoa school."

"You from Pahoa?" Tutu inquired with interest.

"No, I'm from Hilo. If you need transportation, we can send a truck."

"No, I don't need transportation," Tutu told him.

The man glanced doubtfully at their old car. It was a rusting old model that Tutu took out on the road between their farm and the village once a week to buy groceries and on Sundays when they went to church.

Its windows would not roll up — they were cracked, anyway — and the windshield was milky. The car would not go faster than thirty miles an hour.

When she drove it, Tutu leaned out the window to see where she was going, wearing a straw hat with fresh flowers on it to protect her from the sun, tooting the horn sociably at everyone they passed, while Kimo, squeezed in beside her, watched his side of the road for her.

"Take only what you need," the Civil Defense man advised. "Bedding and a change of clothes. Food will be supplied in the cafeteria, and there are cots in the gym. When are you planning to leave?"

"I'm not planning to leave," Tutu said.

The man wiped sweat from his face again. "We strongly advise you not to spend another night here. We can send a truck if you want to take your television set with you."

"*Mahalo,* many thanks," Tutu said amiably. "I don' worry."

"Think about it," he urged. "I'll be back to see you."

"You don' have to worry, either," she told him kindly. "Madame Pele is my friend."

"Of course, Tutu. But just to be on the safe side — ?"

"You think I want to insult her?" she demanded, scorn coming into her tone.

"I see. Well, you may change your mind. Everyone has been ordered out of the village by midnight. It's possible the order will be extended to include this section. In any case, I'll be back."

He walked to his car and backed it expertly down the long lane to the road, while Kimo watched in admiration. But he had left Tutu in a bad mood.

She sniffed and snorted while she prepared supper, saying, as Mrs. Oana had, "What does a *haole* know about these things?"

Kimo remembered some of the things Dr. Gerard had told them. "They have instruments up at the Observatory — " he began doubtfully, but his grandmother did not want to listen.

"After all, we are Pele's people!" she exclaimed. "I'm not going to leave my house!"

After supper, Tutu settled herself in her rocker on

the front porch, while Kimo sat on the steps and threw an old can for Poki to fetch. Poki had a strange fondness for cans and much preferred chasing them to sticks.

They had hardly settled down when the house shook with the strongest tremor Kimo had yet felt. At almost the same time, he noticed a faint orange glow just visible above the trees.

"Look!" he cried.

"*Aia!*" his grandmother exclaimed. It was an Hawaiian expression and it sounded something like "eye-ya!" She pushed her great body up from the rocker. "Madame Pele's at it again!"

Standing where she could see the orange glow, which seemed to jump higher and higher above the trees, she began to chant an old prayer.

Above her rhythmic chanting, Kimo heard a low rumbling noise that was different from the rumble of the surf in the opposite direction. Nor was it like the roar of jets that sometimes streaked across the sky from the air bases on Oahu. It was not like anything Kimo could remember hearing.

It was not steady, but came in short bursts, like a giant cough. The little house shook and rattled with it. From far-off, Kimo heard the whine of a patrol-car siren. Poki stopped chewing on the can and sat on her haunches and howled.

"Get my car keys, Kimo," Tutu said. "We must go and make an offering."

He ran through the trembling house into Tutu's bedroom and snatched her purse. When he came back, Tutu was in the kitchen, wrapping a piece of roast pork in waxed paper. Kimo dug into the purse until he found her keys.

The radio, which Tutu had left on after supper, suddenly began crackling with excited talk. Tutu paused long enough to hear the announcer name the farm nearest the new eruption, then she turned it off.

"Hurry," she urged Kimo, giving him the pork and taking the keys.

Together they went out to the ancient car. Kimo squeezed in the front seat beside Tutu. At first the car would not start, but at last his grandmother got the engine going. Kimo leaned out the window to look back for her but instead of backing out, Tutu jerked the little car forward, made a grand sweeping circle across her front lawn back to the drive and shot out on the road.

Dusk fell quickly as they chugged up from the coast. Soon Kimo could see the shooting red tracers that marked the path of the red-hot rocks being tossed up against the darkening sky.

He thought, in wonder, that it was like New Year's

Eve when their Chinese friends set off firecrackers to frighten away evil spirits as the New Year came in.

Traffic was heavy after they passed the first crossroad. There were cars of all descriptions — National Guard trucks painted a military olive brown, small pickups loaded with boxes and appliances, and automobiles filled with sightseers in a holiday mood. Some carried ukuleles.

When they came to a long line of parked cars, Tutu pulled off behind the last one. Other cars pulled off behind them. Kimo and his grandmother joined a throng of men, women, and children hurrying across a farmyard and through an orchard toward the fountains of lava.

Everyone was excited. Each time there was a spurt of orange lighting the sky, Kimo heard admiring cries out of the darkness ahead of them. Madame Pele's name was on everyone's lips.

"*Ai*, she's on a rampage this time!" Tutu exclaimed. She was in high spirits. "She's going to show folks a few of her tricks now."

And, indeed, she was! There were not one but several fiery fountains shooting flame into the sky and they seemed to grow taller with each burst. Kimo yelled with excitement.

When the crowd thickened and slowed, he

squirmed and pushed his way through it until he reached the very front row of watchers.

Now he could see, through the smoke and fine rain of cinders that was the cooled lava falling back to earth, the silhouettes of men moving about very close to the volcano's new vent. Some carried cameras. Others must be the scientists from the Observatory, for he recognized Dr. Gerard among them.

Only a few yards away was the river of lava, a bright orange stream where it pushed over the lip of the vent, quickly darkening as its surface cooled, then cracking with a noise like breaking dishes. In the cracks it glowed as red as the coals in Mr. Yamasaki's charcoal *hibachi*. A hot river that flowed like cold molasses, it inched its way down the slope toward the canefields.

"Hi!"

Kimo recognized Hiroshi's voice before he turned his head. He waited with loathing for Hiroshi to say, "What did I tell you?"

But instead, Hiroshi said, not like a worst enemy at all, "Great, isn't it? The scientists were the first ones here, did you know that? They're taking samples of everything. I'm going to get a sample too."

Before Kimo could reply, Hiroshi had darted toward the smoking lava. A burst from the volcano lit up his running figure.

"Hey, there, where do you think you're going?" It was Big Dan striding after him. He grabbed Hiroshi by an arm and yanked him back. "Look at you! You've singed your eyebrows!"

"I was just going to get a sample of lava for my collection," Hiroshi protested, trying to wriggle out of the police officer's big hand.

"For your collection, eh?"

Hiroshi nodded. "For my *scientific* collection."

"Give me your stick." Big Dan walked up to a small finger of lava, knocked a smoking rock loose and rolled it across the ground toward Hiroshi. "Let it cool, now," he warned.

He saw Kimo and asked, "Do you want a sample too?"

Just then Kimo saw a familiar small package wrapped in waxed paper come sailing through the air from behind him. It lit on the hot lava, and the paper burst into flames. The smell of burnt pork mingled with the acrid sulphur fumes of the volcano.

A murmur arose from the watchers. "An offering!" someone said, and once again Madame Pele's name was on everyone's lips.

"No," Kimo answered the policeman loudly.

But Big Dan had already gone back for another sample of lava. After it cooled, Kimo thought he might as well pick it up and put it in his pocket.

8

THAT NIGHT Kimo's house rumbled and shook with the bursts of fiery rock exploding from the volcano's new vents. Once again they all slept in one bed.

As soon as it was light, Kimo dressed and went outside. Billowing brown smoke rose above the ridge beyond the orchard, hiding the flaming red that had been so spectacular last night.

Even before he went back into the kitchen to turn the radio on, Kimo knew the canefields were burning. He could smell the burnt sugar in the acrid fumes and fine black ash of the smoke.

"Kimo!" his grandmother called.

"Yes, ma'am?"

"Put the coffee on."

He turned the radio up while he ran water into the coffee pot. The announcer said there were ten fountains spurting lava along the rift that had opened up that day, sending a heavy swift-moving flow of lava along a natural gulley to the sea. A smaller arm of lava was threatening the warm springs. Men with bulldozers were already pushing up enormous dikes of earth to try to save the picnic spot.

"Tutu!"

"I heard," his grandmother said sleepily. "Madame Pele's not going to destroy her favourite spot. Don' worry."

But Kimo could not help it. There was a big lump of worry in his throat. It had been there ever since they had driven to see the lava last night.

The volcano was so awesomely bigger and stronger than he could have imagined that he could not trust Tutu's friend as completely as she did.

He was glad when Big Dan's patrol car turned into their drive.

The police officer got out and came up to the door. "Tutu, have you got some papayas for me this morning?"

Tutu greeted him warmly. "Sure, Dan. What's the matter? You got no papayas over your place any more?"

"The lava crossed my orchard last night. The trees that didn't fall down and burn have cooked papayas hanging on them this morning."

Tutu cried sympathetically, "*Auwe!* That's too bad! How many you want?"

"Two, three."

"Kimo, run get three, four papayas, eh?"

Kimo did not want to go because he suspected that Big Dan had not come for papayas but to try to persuade Tutu to leave. But he had no choice. He ran out through the kitchen, took the long pole with the knife at its tip from its hook beside the door, and hurried into the orchard.

The papayas grew high up under their umbrella of leaves. Kimo cut the stem loose from the trunk with one hand and expertly caught the small melon-like fruit with the other, then laid it carefully on the ground.

When he had gathered four or five, so Big Dan could choose the ones he wanted, he hooked the knife into the pale trunk of the tree to return for it later. With his arms full of papayas, he hurried back to the house.

Big Dan was wiping his forehead just as the man from Hilo had done, saying, "Let us know if you change your mind, Tutu. That ridge is protecting you now, but for how long?"

"Don' worry," Tutu said comfortably.

"I'll carry these to the car for you," Kimo offered.

Big Dan smiled at him. "Okay."

As they walked, a plane flew low overhead. The officer looked up at it and sighed. "Sightseers from

Honolulu. The sky will be filled with them today."

When Kimo had put the papayas on the floor of the car, he asked, "Is Madame Pele a real goddess, Big Dan?"

The officer looked at him thoughtfully before answering. "More like a witch," he said then. "A mischievous witch who likes to play tricks on people. When she is angry, her tricks are wicked and vengeful. Have you heard the story about the chiefs she challenged to a *holua* race?"

Kimo shook his head. "Tutu didn't tell me that one."

"You've heard how, in the old days, the chiefs amused themselves sliding down the wet grasses of the mountainside, standing like a surfer on their *holua* sleds? Well, one day Pele made herself into a beautiful young girl and challenged some young chiefs to a race. She could ride a sled almost as good as a man, but the chiefs rode faster.

"This made her angry, and when Pele lost her temper the grass burned and the earth shook. She said, 'Let's race again!' But the young men were afraid of her now, and tried to run away.

"That made her angrier. Her eyes shot lightning. Her breath smoked. She threw flames after them. They raced for the sea where they planned to escape in a canoe.

"But Pele changed herself into a river of fire that sped down the mountain after them. Pele won that race."

He pointed to the old lava ridge beyond the orchard. "Some say that is the trail she left. You know those mounds of rock down by the beach? Some say that's where she overtook the chiefs and buried them in lava."

"*Ai!*" Kimo cried, shivering with excitement. "Do you know any more stories about Pele, Big Dan?"

"Lots of them, but I've got to go now."

"I'm collecting evidence about her," Kimo explained.

The officer put his hand in his pocket. "Here's

some evidence for you. These are Pele's tears. She tossed them out of the volcano."

Kimo closed his hand over the tear-shaped bits of black volcanic glass. They were as smooth and shiny as pearls. "*Mahalo*, thank you!" he cried.

Now he had something besides stories for evidence!

"I want you to promise me two things, Kimo. One, that you won't go out collecting evidence about Madame Pele alone. Two, that you will try to persuade your *tutu* to take you to Pahoa school. Okay?"

Kimo studied Big Dan's gentle dark face.

"I don't trust Pele," Big Dan said soberly. Then he added, "The men up at the Observatory say their instruments show that the accumulation of lava beneath the volcano is almost ten times what it was before the last eruption."

"Is it dangerous to stay here?"

"It could become dangerous, if the lava flow increases rapidly enough to top that ridge. But even before that, there is the danger it will cut off your escape roads."

Kimo nodded.

"I'll be back." Big Dan started his motor. Tutu was still standing on her porch, and he called, "Better change your mind, Tutu! I'd hate to have to carry you out. Might have to use a wheelbarrow!"

"I'm not that big, Danny!" Tutu retorted and laughed at what she considered a fine compliment.

Kimo went thoughtfully back to the house. Big Dan had given him much to think about.

"Is Madame Pele a goddess or a witch?" he asked his grandmother.

"A witch!" she exclaimed. "Where do you get such notions? Is that what Dan was telling you?"

"Well, is she a goddess then?"

"She's a spirit," Tutu said angrily, "and our ancestor. We are Pele's people! Somebody's gone too far an' made her angry. Some peoples got to change their greedy ways, tha's what!" She went about her housework, muttering to herself about the wickedness of those who had forgotten the old traditions of sharing the bounty of the land.

9

THE SCHOOL BUS WAS not coming today. Kimo did not know when it would come again. He felt lost and lonely and kept saying, "I wish there was something to do," until Tutu began to get very annoyed with him.

He went out in the yard then and tried to see Madame Pele in the brown smoke and white steam billowing up above the banana and papaya trees, but he did not know whether he was looking for a young girl or an old woman. He did not see anything like either one in the rolling smoke turning itself inside out as it rose from the volcano.

The house rattled and shook, and the sky grew blacker. All morning cars went by on the road, going empty one way, returning loaded with people and their belongings.

At ten o'clock the radio was saying only a half dozen families remained in the area, but farmers were still returning to feed their stock and to bring out more possessions. The village, the radio said, had been completely evacuated by midnight last night.

A little later, it reported the fountains had stopped.

"You see?" Tutu said, and turned off the radio, but not before Kimo had heard the man say continuing "harmonic tremors" indicated to the Observatory scientists that lava was still moving underneath the region.

Tutu was concerned about Mrs. Kealoha's chickens. Hanalei's mother had not returned to feed them. "Her hens will stop laying if they're not fed," Tutu said. "I'm going to take some feed over to them."

While she was gone, there was an explosion from the direction of the volcano, and white steam billowed up through the dark smoke. The explosive bursts continued, accompanied by sounds like a great coughing. The volcano was erupting again!

Kimo was about to run in and turn the radio on when he saw the Yamasaki car coming slowly up the road, heavily loaded. Tokiko waved at him, and he waved back.

Mr. Yamasaki slowed his car still more and turned in at Tutu's drive. Kimo ran up. The car radio was broadcasting news of the eruption.

"Where is your grandmother?"

"She's feeding Mrs. Kealoha's hens. Are you going to Pahoa school?"

"Yes, we've had it!" Mrs. Yamasaki exclaimed. "You and your grandmother better leave too."

"Tutu says we're safe here."

"This new flow is heavy and coming fast," Mr. Yamasaki told him. "We just heard the lava has already overflowed the dike they pushed up to protect the springs."

"Yes!" Tokiko exclaimed tearfully. "The trees are burning, and lava is flowing into the pool."

Kimo could hardly believe it. Tutu had been so sure Madame Pele would spare her favourite bathing spot.

"I wish you would come with us," Tokiko urged.

How he wished he could! "I have to stay with Tutu, but I will send Poki and Fluff with you," he offered.

"Can I take them?" Tokiko asked her mother.

Her mother looked at her father.

"There's bound to be a place set up for pets," Mr. Yamasaki said after a moment. "I'll tell you what, Kimo. We'll take them if you will ride along to help with them. I am coming back to feed my cows when I get my family settled, and you can come back with me."

"Have you a leash for Poki?" Tokiko's mother asked.

"Yes." Kimo ran and got it. "Here, Poki!" he called. "Do you want to go for a ride?"

Poki did not have many invitations to ride and she was quite willing to get into the car when Kimo handed Tokiko the leash. But Fluff was of a different mind. She let Kimo pick her up, but when he tried to take her into the crowded back seat where Tokiko sat with her brother and sister and Poki, Fluff became alarmed.

She struggled out of Kimo's arms, and Tokiko, trying to grab her, got a deep scratch across the back of her hand. Her scream of pain terrified the cat. Fluff bounded for the house and disappeared under the front porch.

Kimo ran after her, but she paid no attention to his coaxing, crouching down with all four paws folded underneath her, just out of his reach.

"Please, Fluff, pretty Fluff, come here!"

She gazed at him with green, unwinking eyes and mewed an answer, but she did not budge from her retreat.

Mr. Yamasaki honked his horn. "I'm afraid we'll have to leave her, Kimo," he called. "Come on, if you want to go with us."

Reluctantly, Kimo left Fluff and climbed in beside Tokiko, taking Poki's leash from her hands.

Poki ran back and forth from one side of the car to the other in her excitement, not caring where she put her feet. Everyone was yelling at her.

"Yuka, you come up front," her mother told Tokiko's sister.

The little girl clambered over the seat, and there was more room. Mr. Yamasaki stopped at the Kealoha house and honked at Tutu to tell her Kimo was with them and drove on.

When they reached the village, taking the detour around the cracked street, they found everything covered by a layer of purplish volcanic ash and cinders, even weeds edging the road.

"Roll up the windows, children," Mrs. Yamasaki said.

At the grocery store, men were carrying cartons to a truck. Nearby a police officer and several other men stood beside a patrol car.

The sounds from the fountains of lava were thunderous, even though there were two low ridges between them and the village.

"At least the school is safe," said Mrs. Yamasaki. "The lava isn't flowing that way."

"It could," said Mr. Yamasaki. "Who knows where it will end?"

Tokiko's mother was silent. They drove on.

Kimo kept looking back at the bursts of lava. A little further on, he cried, "Look! There's a fire engine down there!"

Mr. Yamasaki looked. Then, with an exclamation, he put on his brakes. He turned down a side road and drove toward the farmhouse where the fire truck and several other vehicles were parked.

A small arm of lava about twelve feet high was moving from the volcano into the hollow where the farmhouse stood. The fire truck and a yellow tank truck were both spraying the smoking, steaming hill with water.

Mr. Yamasaki parked the car. "They're trying to stop the flow by cooling the lava so it will harden into rock," he explained.

For a while it seemed to be working. Then the trucks and the firefighters moved back. In another few minutes, the house burst into flames.

Mr. Yamasaki turned the car around and drove back to the Pahoa road. But Kimo got up on his knees on the seat to watch through the rear window.

The mountain of lava scarcely seemed to be moving, yet in a few minutes its weight was pushing in the burning walls and beginning to bury what was left of the house.

When he turned around, Mrs. Yamasaki was looking back with tears in her eyes. "I wonder if we will lose our home too?"

"Don't borrow trouble!" said her husband.

But Kimo could see his face in the rear-view mirror, and he thought Mr. Yamasaki looked anxious too.

10

When they reached Pahoa, the erupting fountains were a great smoking wound in the forested slopes below them. Big Dan was directing the traffic jammed at the entrance to the school.

He waved them into the yard where the yellow busses were usually parked, crowded now with vehicles of all kinds — private cars and National Guard trucks unloading evacuées and their personal possessions, a jeep, and numerous pickups.

Mr. Yamasaki was given directions by a young man in a National Guard uniform and waited his turn to pull up to the gym.

"Four children, Mr. Yamasaki?" asked the lady wearing a Red Cross uniform who was checking in the families.

"Three. Kimo lives next door. He will be back later with his grandmother. Right, Kimo?"

He hesitated. "I think so."

"I see," said the lady. She asked for the names and wrote Kimo's and Tutu's down in a separate column.

A man took Poki's leash. "We'll see that she's taken care of," he told Kimo.

"Did you bring any bedding, Mrs. Yamasaki?"

"Yes. Tokiko, you can help me make the beds. Kimo, will you help Mr. Yamasaki carry our suitcases in?"

"Yes, ma'am."

The gym looked very different today than it had when Kimo had come here to basketball games. Instead of bleachers, cots were lined up in rows several deep all around the room. Lounging on them were women and children of all ages and a few very old men. Some were playing cards, others were watching a television set in the corner. On one cot sat a mynah bird in a cage who whistled and called "Hello!" with his head cocked first on one side, then the other.

When they had unloaded the car and settled the Yamasaki family on the cots assigned to them, Mr. Yamasaki said, "Come with me, Kimo. I want to stop in at the office and see what's happening."

An odd-looking vehicle was parked outside the entrance to the school basement where the Civil Defense headquarters sign was posted. The National Guardsman standing beside it was talking into a microphone.

"That's the mobile radio shack," Mr. Yamasaki told Kimo as they passed. "He's talking to one of the radio jeeps out in the field."

"What are the jeeps doing?"

"Keeping watch on the flow, giving evacuation orders, calling for trucks, firefighters, the ambulance, or whatever help is needed."

Through the office door, Kimo saw Miss Prince at one of the desks. Across from her, two men were talking into telephones. Several men were standing before a large map on the wall, pointing to the area where the volcano was erupting and talking together. Mr. Yamasaki joined them.

Kimo followed him through the door, then slipped quietly along the wall, hoping no one would see him and tell him to run along.

"Hey, look where you're going!" a familiar voice whispered as he stumbled against something.

He looked down and saw Hiroshi squatting on his heels against the wall. Hiroshi motioned him down with an urgent gesture, and Kimo obeyed.

"This is a good place to be," Hiroshi whispered. "Everybody comes here, all the scientists, the reporters from Honolulu, everybody!" His eyes were snapping bright, and his whisper crackled with excitement. Now and then he wiggled his ears.

"Look what I've got for my collection!" he said and reached into his pocket for a small box. Carefully, he opened it. Inside Kimo saw some fine strands of what looked like glass.

"What is it?"

"Pele's hair."

"Pele's hair!"

"That's what it's called," Hiroshi said, looking a little sheepish. "It came out of the volcano."

Gingerly, Kimo touched it. It felt like glass — glass spun as fine as hair. He reached into his own pocket and as casually as he could manage, pulled out the shiny black pearls Big Dan had given him.

Hiroshi's eyes popped with excitement. *"Lapilli!"*

"Pele's tears!" Kimo said, glaring at him.

Hiroshi swallowed and nodded. "The geologists call them lapilli," he said almost apologetically. He picked one out of Kimo's hand and held one of his strands of glassy hair up to it. "When they come out of the volcano there's a strand of Pele's hair trailing from the thin end, like this." They looked at each other in wonder.

"I haven't got any of those. I don't s-suppose — " Hiroshi was beginning to stutter. "H-how about swapping a few?" He pulled out a glassy smooth piece of lava. "*Pahoehoe,*" he offered.

Kimo shook his head. Real smooth *pahoehoe* was harder to find than the common spongy *aa* lava, but there was still plenty of it. "I'm just collecting Pele's things," he explained.

Hiroshi hesitated, looking at his strands of glassy hair and then enviously at Kimo's black pearls. From another pocket he pulled some dark green stones. "*Olivines,*" he said. "Some people call these Hawaiian diamonds."

Kimo shook his head.

Abruptly, Hiroshi gave in. "All right."

Kimo picked out two gleaming tears, neither the largest nor the smallest, and received a generous wad of Pele's hair in exchange for them.

"Man!" Hiroshi exclaimed in delight, and Kimo could not help smiling.

"Listen!" Hiroshi nudged him.

The men over by the map were talking about the earthen dikes that were being bulldozed up to try to save the village. "They will be useless in a flow of this magnitude," one of them argued.

"If we build them big enough — "

"If they hold, a lava lake will build up behind them. With an internal temperature of around two thousand degrees, it could have a greater potential for damage than the original flow!"

"Maybe we should try to move the school buildings," another suggested. "How much time do we have?"

"At last reports, the lava was moving about twenty feet an hour."

Miss Prince rose from her desk to go to a file and saw Kimo and Hiroshi. "Hello, boys. Have you moved into the gym?"

"Yes, ma'am," said Hiroshi.

"No, ma'am," said Kimo.

She stopped, her smile turning quizzical. Just then Mr. Yamasaki came up.

"Ready, Kimo?" He smiled and greeted their teacher.

"Do you have your family here, Mr. Yamasaki?" she asked.

"Yes. Now I am going back for some of our possessions."

Miss Prince frowned. "I'm afraid you can't go now. That road has been blocked, except to cars coming out of the area."

"No!" Mr. Yamasaki turned to the desk where one of the Civil Defense officers had just put down his telephone. He confirmed what Miss Prince had said.

"The order was given because of choked traffic conditions and because the fumes and falling cinders in the village are now so heavy as to be a hazard. We have many sightseers trying to get to the volcano, and these inexperienced people can be overcome by the fumes before they realize it."

"But I am not a sightseer!" Mr. Yamasaki protested heatedly. "I must feed my stock and bring out more clothes and things for my family!"

"The restrictions may be lifted for those who live in the area when the wind changes direction. Check with us again."

Kimo pressed forward until he stood at the desk.

"My *tutu* is still at home," he said urgently. "I've got to get back to her."

"Where does your *tutu* live?"

"On Pohai road."

"Someone will bring her out. We have wardens in there, checking to make sure everyone leaves the dangerous zones." His phone rang, and he turned back to answer it.

Kimo thought despairingly that no warden could persuade Tutu if she did not want to come out. What was he to do?

Miss Prince put a hand lightly on his shoulder. "You're with friends here. Are you hungry? You can get milk in the cafeteria, you know."

He shook his head. Despondently, he went back to Hiroshi who was still squatting against the wall, his bright eyes taking everything in.

They watched and listened as reports came in from the volcano and the black outline of lava on the map on the wall widened and crept closer to the sea. They heard of a farmer's house that burned, of another whose roof collapsed from the weight of falling cinders.

They were so quiet and unmoving that the busy adults forgot they were there. They listened to a telephone conversation with the Humane Society in Hilo about abandoned animals in the disaster area and to a report by Dr. Gerard on the continuing seismic tremors that indicated the end of the eruption was not yet in sight.

Hiroshi was utterly absorbed in what they were seeing and hearing, but Kimo's mind was like a bird trying to get out of a cage, flying this way and that as he wondered what in the world he could do about his grandmother, whose stubborn faith in her friend, Madame Pele, had him really worried.

They were still squatting there when a smoke-grimed warden came in from the field to consult with the Civil Defense director. The director was talking to some government officials who had flown over from Honolulu. While the warden waited his turn,

Miss Prince poured him a cup of coffee from the urn in the corner.

"Is everybody out of your sector?" Kimo heard her ask him.

"Everyone but that old *tutu* on Pohai road. She won't budge. Ordered me off her property!"

"That's my *tutu*," Kimo said under his breath to Hiroshi. They inched along the wall until they were closer.

"She said, 'I'm tired of you fellows coming around yakkity-yakking. Next time, I'll talk with my shotgun!' "

Miss Prince gasped and laughed. "Did she mean it?"

"How do I know? I left. She's in a 'voluntary evacuation' zone. If she doesn't want to leave, I can't make her."

"I believe they are putting out an official evacuation order because of the fumes and heavy ash fallout extending that way."

"I would have to take two men and an ambulance to evacuate her by force. She must weigh three hundred pounds!"

"And she's strong!" Kimo said. He had been unable to stay quiet, against the wall. "That's my *tutu*," he told Miss Prince.

"Does she really have a gun?" the warden asked him.

"Yes." It was an old gun that belonged to his grandfather. For many years now it had stood in the closet in Tutu's room. "I don't know if she has shells for it," he added, as they looked at each other. "Will you take me back there with you?" he asked the warden.

"I'm afraid I can't do that."

"You're with the Yamasakis, aren't you?" Miss Prince asked him.

"Yes, but Mr. Yamasaki was going to take me right back."

"You're better off here," his teacher said. "Don't worry about your grandmother. We'll take care of her."

"She's in no immediate danger," the warden added. He glanced at the desk where the director was still busy. "I'm going over to the cafeteria and get something to eat," he told Miss Prince. "I'll be back."

Kimo went back to Hiroshi. He was very worried. "I've just got to get back to Tutu."

"Well, let's go," Hiroshi said matter-of-factly.

"How?"

"Come on," said his worst enemy, who did not seem so much of an enemy now.

11

As THEY PASSED an open door, Hiroshi took Kimo's arm. "Hey, let's go look at the seismograph!"

"Not now!"

But Hiroshi pulled him into the room. "Hello, Dr. Gerard," he said eagerly.

The scientist looked up from the apparatus mounted on concrete in the centre of the room. "Hello, boys. Want to see an earthquake?"

"Yes!"

Kimo followed Hiroshi over and looked down through the glass at the squiggly line being drawn on the revolving drum. He said, "I can't feel any earthquake."

"The seismograph is so delicate it registers many tremors we cannot feel. It looks like that arm, attached to the weights, is moving, doesn't it? Actually, the weights are standing still but the earth is moving beneath them."

"Are you going to change the paper on the drum?" Hiroshi asked, when the arm was drawing a straight line again.

"Yes." Dr. Gerard opened the glass case and removed the lined paper. "See, the paper is timed so we can tell when the tremors occurred. And by comparing the size of the squiggles on other records from our network of seismograph stations, we can tell where the tremors were strongest and by mathematics figure the point deep below the earth's surface where they started."

"What else do you do at the Observatory?"

"Well, we make a daily summary of these records and publish the summaries in a quarterly bulletin. They help us predict — "

"When an eruption is coming?" Hiroshi interrupted in his eagerness.

"No, when one *could* take place. The prediction in days and weeks is still far off." He punched Hiroshi lightly. "Some young fellow like you may be the first to do that."

Hiroshi glowed. "But first I have to go to college."

"All the way to the top. A doctor's degree."

Hiroshi would have just stood there asking questions forever, Kimo thought impatiently. But Dr. Gerard put the seismograph record in his equipment bag and strode out. They followed him up into the sunshine.

The scientist paused at the mobile radio shack.

"The lava is only a few feet from the coast, sir," said the soldier holding the microphone.

Dr. Gerard nodded and hurried toward a waiting jeep, which a driver had kept running.

"Hey, ask him if we can go with him!" Kimo shouted.

Dr. Gerard heard and laughed. "No passengers," he said and waved as the jeep took off.

"He could have taken us through the road block," Kimo told Hiroshi, disappointed.

"He may not even be going that way," Hiroshi said, important with superior knowledge. "He's maybe going somewhere to take a boat or a plane so he can watch the lava fall over the cliffs into the water."

Kimo was getting desperate. "Well, I've got to get home if I have to walk."

"Somebody would stop you. We've got to have a plan."

Just then Tokiko ran up to them, her black hair bouncing. "Where have you been? I looked all over for you."

"Oh, around," Kimo told her.

"I went to see how Poki likes being penned up. She was sure glad to see me," Tokiko reported happily. "That man who took her is from the Humane Society in Hilo."

"The dog catcher?" Kimo said in surprise.

She nodded, making her hair bounce again. "He said lots of people had to just walk off and leave their animals. He and another man are going back and rescue them. So maybe he will rescue Fluff, if your *tutu* doesn't bring her."

"I don't think Fluff will come for Tutu."

"Well, you'd better tell him about Fluff," Tokiko said. "That's his car right over there."

Kimo and Hiroshi both looked at the panel truck she pointed out. "I don't think Fluff would come for him, either."

"He said he was going back there, huh?" Hiroshi spoke slowly.

Tokiko nodded. "Maybe if you could go with him?"

"Just what I was thinking." Hiroshi nudged Kimo. "Come on."

They found the dog catcher talking to a man in a National Guard uniform. "Check with our radio jeep when you get in the area," the soldier was telling him, "so we will know where you are and can warn you if you should have to get out in a hurry."

"Okay," said the dog catcher. He started to get in beside the other man driving the truck.

"Can we go with you?" Hiroshi asked him.

"No kids," said the soldier. "Run along."

"Please," Kimo begged. "I want to get my cat."

The dog catcher paused, holding the cab door open. "We'll get your cat. Where is it?"

"She's under my house and won't come out for anybody else."

"Don't worry about that. They all come to us when they get hungry. Where do you live?"

"On Pohai road next to Yamasaki's."

"I know where that is. We'll get her." He started a second time to climb into the truck.

"The doors are not closed," said the driver, who was looking in his rear-view mirror.

The dog catcher went around the truck and closed them. Kimo and Hiroshi followed him and watched as he latched the panel doors. There was only a little pane of glass high on each door.

His driver had the motor going, but this time when the dog catcher started to climb in beside him, a National Guardsman brought him a message from the mobile radio shack.

"Quick!" Hiroshi cried and opened the doors again.

Tokiko came running up. "What are you going to do?"

"Be quiet!" Hiroshi told her sharply. Kimo was already climbing into the truck. Inside, it was piled high with empty crates and boxes. There were so many of them Kimo could hardly find room enough to sit.

Hiroshi pulled the doors to, but there was no latch on the inside. "Shut us in!" he told Tokiko, who was standing staring up at them with her mouth open. "Quick!"

"And don't tell anybody," Kimo warned.

She looked first one way, then the other. Just when Kimo had decided she was going to call her father, she swiftly closed and fastened the doors.

Now they were locked in!

"I hope you know what we're doing," he muttered to Hiroshi, as the truck began to move.

12

THE TRUCK ROLLED slowly out of the school yard and turned into the road. On the other side of the grid that separated the back from the front seat, the two men were talking. Kimo, squatting among the boxes, did not make a sound. Neither did Hiroshi.

It was hard to tell in what direction they were going, crouched there in the dark. Kimo was pretty sure they were headed for the volcano, although he could not be absolutely sure until they stopped at the road block. He recognized the voice that greeted their driver. It was Big Dan's.

"Going after abandoned animals? Don't stop in the village. We've had to pull everybody out of there because the fallout was heavy enough to cause some injuries. Check with our radio jeep."

"Okay." The driver shifted gears and the truck moved on.

Presently, above the rumbling cough of the volcano, Kimo could hear the rain of cinders bouncing like marbles off the truck's metal roof. The air was hot and smoky and it made his eyes smart. His throat felt dry, and the taste of ashes was in his mouth.

Now the truck made so many turns that Kimo lost all sense of direction. Often they bounced over rough roads. Hiroshi's eyes were shiny bright in the dusky interior of the truck.

They stopped again, but though the men were shouting over the explosive roar of the volcano, Kimo could not hear what was said.

"Must be the radio jeep," he whispered.

Hiroshi said nothing. He just kept looking at Kimo with that shining excitement in his eyes.

When they moved on, the air began to clear, and the sounds of the volcano grew more distant. The truck made another turn and came to a stop. A dog began barking.

The driver jumped down. Before Kimo had time even to duck his head, the back doors of the panel truck were thrown open and he was looking into the surprised face of the dog catcher's assistant.

"Well, son-a-ma-gun!"

The dog catcher came around from the other side of the truck. "What's this? Some stowaways?"

The assistant was plainly irritated. "I thought we told you two to get lost! What'll we do with them?" he asked his boss. "Take them back to Pahoa?"

"As long as they're here, let's put them to work. We can use some extra hands." He turned to Kimo. "You're worried about your cat, eh? We'll get over that way pretty soon. Right now, you boys get in that henhouse over there and get every last hen into this crate." He tossed it at them, and they caught it awkwardly between them.

"Yes, sir," Hiroshi said.

Kimo followed Hiroshi into the henhouse. He did not see what else he could do.

The hens set up a squawking and a flapping of their wings that was the worst racket Kimo had ever heard. He shut the door of the coop behind him so they could not get out.

Hiroshi had led the way purposefully, but now that they were inside he looked quite helpless.

"You grab them by the legs," Kimo told him. "Like this." Mrs. Kealoha had taught him how once when she offered Tutu a hen for their supper.

One by one, they got the panicky hens by the legs and thrust them into the crate, managing somehow to keep from being pecked. It was not easy.

"Ever notice you can't hold a chicken upside-down?" Kimo panted, struggling with a hefty hen. Try as he might to put her in head first, she always managed to stretch her neck around to keep her head out of the crate.

Hiroshi was sneezing from chicken dust. "A volcanologist would never have to catch hens!" he said in disgust.

Kimo felt the same way, but he told himself if they had to catch hens, they had to catch hens.

Finally they had the last one. They closed the crate and carried it between them out into the yard. The wary, barking dog had been lured into a trap and was growling with pleasure as he chewed on a meaty bone, too hungry to care that he was being shut into a box.

The men marked the crates with the owner's name, loaded them, put Kimo and Hiroshi between

them on the front seat, and drove to the next abandoned farm.

It was a place Kimo had visited with his grandmother and it seemed strange to see no one about but a lean, hungry dog who crept out from under the front porch and came toward them barking half-heartedly and wagging his tail.

A curtain stirred in an open window. Through it Kimo could see the table with a pineapple sitting on a plate just as the woman of the house had left it. At the door was a pair of *zoris,* the sandals the Japanese farmer had kicked off before entering his house.

They trapped the hungry dog and drove on.

They were working closer and closer to a fire burning in the forest. At one place, Kimo glimpsed the twenty-foot high wall of lava that was burning the trees in its path. Silhouetted against the flames, half obscured by smoke, were some dark figures.

"Hey, those sightseers are close!" Kimo yelled.

"No sightseers in here now," said the dog catcher. "The show is over. Those men over there are the scientists, keeping their fingers on Pele's pulse."

" 'Keeping their fingers on Pele's pulse'?" Kimo repeated hopefully.

"It's just an expression," said the dog catcher.

Hiroshi did not say anything. Kimo appreciated that.

Before they reached Pohai road, they came to the small pink church in the forest where Tutu brought him to worship on Sundays. The houses on each side and across the road from it had been abandoned, and they stopped to walk around them and through the churchyard, looking for stray animals.

"If the eruption doesn't let up soon, the church will go," said the dog catcher. "It's right in the path of the flow."

Kimo felt a tightness in his chest just thinking about it. He looked at the column of brown smoke boiling up into the sky above the trees. Then he looked at the little church, its red roof made drab by cinders. Above the entry was an inscription in Hawaiian that meant "This is God's house." Tutu loved to come here because it was one of the few churches where the hymns were still sung in Hawaiian.

Surely Madame Pele would not burn their church!

All at once Kimo had the cold feeling that there was not any Madame Pele at all, that Hiroshi and Dr. Gerard and Miss Prince were right about the volcano, and that his grandmother was deceived.

There was no friend in whom she could trust. She had no one but him, Kimo. He had to go home and help her to understand that she must escape the fury of the volcano before it was too late.

13

In the back of the truck now were thirty hens, four dogs, seven cats, and a goat. The cats were all crying, and the goat was bleating. Now and then one of the dogs growled, but the frightened hens made hardly a sound as the truck bounced along.

The driver had turned off on a road that took them to the sea, dark grey under the smoke-filled sky. Kimo looked up at the volcano. The cones of cinders piling up around the fountains as the burst of lava fell back to earth were higher than the tallest trees, giant pimples on the mountain's cheek.

As they rounded a point, they could see, beyond a stretch of rocky coast, the great white clouds of steam rising from the ocean as the hot river of lava rolled over a cliff and dropped into the water.

"See that, boys?" the dog catcher said. "It's changing the map of the island. In twenty years, somebody will be growing papayas on that point of new land piling up there on the beach."

"That's the way our island was built," Hiroshi volunteered, eager as always to show off his knowledge. "Yeah, we're lucky in some ways. Our volcanoes keep chucking up new real estate for us."

Kimo listened, saying nothing, worrying about his grandmother. He wondered if someone had persuaded her to leave, if they would find her gone when they came to his house.

Around the next bend in the road they met a jeep. In it were Dr. Gerard and his assistant. The dog catcher pulled up in the road, and the jeep stopped beside him.

"Hello, Dr. Gerard. You been to bed yet?"

"Not yet," the scientist said smiling.

"A long time without sleep, isn't it?"

"It will soon be forty-eight hours."

"You fellas must save up all your work for an eruption."

"It gives us such a fine opportunity for research that we must use twenty-four hours in every day."

"Any signs of a let-up?" the dog catcher asked.

"I wish there were. The flow is still heavy. Lava lakes have filled the pit calderas — "

"What's that?" Hiroshi interrupted.

"The craters. Magma is also beginning to build up behind the lava cooled by the ocean. This is widening the flow and threatening areas on each side of it. We have one stream of fast-flowing *pahoehoe* moving toward the village. The bulldozers are in there now, pushing up a dike between it and the school. They will keep a road open for you."

"Thanks, Doc," they said, and the driver went on.

At the next farmhouse, a telephone company truck was parked out in the yard. As they drove in, a repairman came out of the house with a telephone in his hand, coiling its wires around it.

"Must be expecting the lava here," the driver said.

Back on the road, a truck went by them carrying pots of orchid plants. Beside its driver sat Mr. Yamasaki's father. Kimo had visited his orchid farm with Tokiko. Mrs. Yamasaki had said that day that the old gentleman was as fond of his orchids as he was of his grandchildren. Kimo was glad they were being rescued.

At last they turned in from the coast and drove on Pohai road. "That's my house!" Kimo cried pointing. But he was shocked at the change in it since this morning. The grass and all of Tutu's flowers were turned a purplish grey with cinder and ash. A grey layer of cinders had piled up like icing on the roof.

When they first turned in the long drive, he thought his grandmother must have left. Then he realized the reason it was so quiet. It was because Poki was not there to run, barking, to meet him.

He watched for Tutu to step to the door with her welcoming *"Aloha!"* But the house was still. Yet Kimo knew it was not empty.

He had noticed something that told him Tutu was home. The rocker on the front porch was swaying gently, as it did when she had just lifted her great body out of it.

Then he noticed something else. The screen door was beginning slowly to open. In the next instant there was a thunderous explosion. Shot whistled by the truck. The driver slammed on his brakes and yelled.

"That *pupule wahine* is shooting at us!"

For an instant after that, the cab of the truck was so still Kimo could hear himself breathe. He could see the barrel of his grandfather's old shotgun protruding from the doorway and could barely make out Tutu's huge outline behind the screen.

"Who is she?"

"My *tutu.* She's old and stubborn, but she's not a crazy woman!

"She's been drinking a toast to Madame Pele," Kimo said, and his throat felt thick with tears.

"This is a matter for the police," the dog catcher said. "It's not our problem. Let's go find the radio jccp."

The driver put the truck in reverse. Quick as a

flash, Kimo grabbed the door handle. As he jumped, the dog catcher reached for him. Kimo was almost sure Hiroshi deliberately got in the man's way.

He shouted, "It's me, Tutu!" and landed on the grass running.

"Come back here, you *pupule* kid!" the dog catcher shouted.

Kimo, streaking for the house, paid no attention. When he leaped on the porch, Fluff came flying from somewhere, and he stumbled over her as she ran between his legs. His grandmother grabbed him and thrust him behind her, still holding the gun.

"Get off my land!" she shouted at the truck.

"Don't shoot," Kimo begged her. "It's the dog catcher from Hilo. I've been helping him rescue the animals."

"I don' care who he is!"

"He gave me a ride — "

"I'm warning you!" she shouted again, over the gun barrel. Kimo heard the truck shift gears. When he looked around his grandmother's restraining arm, the truck was backing out of the drive.

"Coming here all the time yakkity-yakking! I told them I was tired of yakking!"

But Kimo, watching the panel truck disappear with Hiroshi still in the cab, felt suddenly very much alone.

14

TUTU LEANED her gun against the door frame. "What you want to eat?" she asked Kimo. "Shall I fix you something to eat?"

"I'm not hungry," Kimo said miserably.

"Well, you'd better give that cat some milk."

Tutu was probably right, because Fluff was rubbing against his legs. When he had the milk out, he poured a glass for himself too and sat at the kitchen table to drink it while he thought about his problem.

They could not spend another night in this rattling, shaking house with the volcano raining ashes on them. He had to persuade Tutu to leave the house before nightfall. He did not know how he was going to do it, but he had to find a way.

But first he had to do something about his grandfather's gun. Maybe he could hide it. Or shoot all her shells. He got up and walked quietly toward it.

Tutu, who had rcturned to the front porch, called, "Kimo, you leave that gun alone!"

He stood at the screen door. "I didn't know you had any shells for it, Tutu."

"No reason for you to know!"

"Have you got any more?"

"Sure I got more."

"How many?"

"Why you want to know?"

"Can I shoot it?"

"No!" his grandmother said.

Kimo went back to the kitchen. He would have to make another plan. Meanwhile, there was something else he had to do.

He went out in the back yard and found a wooden crate and made a cover with a loose board in it like the ones the dog catcher had. Then he took it into the kitchen where Fluff, who had finished her milk, was daintily licking her paw and washing her face with it.

He picked the cat up and put her in the crate and fastened the loose board so she could not crawl out. Fluff thought it was a game and kept reaching her paw between the boards for his hand.

When he finished, he picked up his milk and went out on the front porch. His grandmother was drinking another toast to Madame Pele. The day looked unnaturally dark, and the porch trembled, and the windows behind them rattled with the rumbles coming from the volcano.

"We came by the church, Tutu. The cinders are about a foot deep on the roof."

"Our church?"

"Yes."

"How deep?" she questioned him sharply.

Kimo measured a foot with his hands.

"Somebody better shovel those cinders off, or the roof will fall in," she said anxiously.

"Everybody's gone to Pahoa."

His grandmother began rocking back and forth.

"The lava's almost to the church," Kimo told her.

"So Pele wants our church!" It was the first time his grandmother had failed to give her friend the title of Madame. "She's really mad at some peoples down here."

Kimo sipped his milk. His grandmother rocked a little faster, watching the brown smoke curling up above the trees and muttering to herself.

After a moment, she exclaimed aloud, "She's going too far!"

"Who, Tutu?"

But she would not say that she was disappointed in her friend. She rocked and muttered and asked irritably, "What's that cat crying for?"

"I think she wants to get out of the box."

"Well, let her out." When Kimo did not move, she demanded, "What have you got her in a box for?"

"So she can be rescued," Kimo said.

Tutu rocked harder. After a little, she burst out, "Pele's got no business harming our church. That's not right. She's got no business down here, anyway! She should have stayed in Kilauea!"

Kimo meditated over his milk. "Tutu," he said, "if Madame Pele is your friend, can't you ask her to spare the church?"

"I offered her pork," Tutu said, rocking angrily. "When the *ohia* blossoms in the spring, I make an offering of *lehua*. In the fall, I give her the first *ohelo* berries. What more does she want? She is punishing some peoples for something!"

Kimo kept still. She rocked harder. "All right!" she said finally. Grasping the bottle beside her with one hand, she pushed herself up from her chair. "Get my car keys, Kimo."

He jumped up and flew into the bedroom for Tutu's purse, stopping on his way back through the kitchen to pick up Fluff's box. He dashed ahead of Tutu to the car and put Fluff into the back seat. Then he climbed in the front, dug in Tutu's purse for her keys, and put the right one in the ignition for her.

Tutu tucked the bottle under her arm and followed him, her long red *muumuu* sweeping the grass.

She had a little trouble starting the car, and Fluff cried piteously in the back seat, but finally they were on their way. Tutu drove straight to the church.

All the houses they passed along the way were deserted, with the black breath of the volcano hanging over them. The air was hot and still, the wilting trees weighed down with ash and cinders. Tutu clucked and exclaimed at each turn of the road.

When they reached the church, they could see the hot smoking mountain that was advancing through the forest toward it. Tutu parked the car. Her usually amiable face was majestically grim.

"I want to talk to Pele alone," she told Kimo.

He stayed in the car and watched her walk toward the lava. She stood erect before it, and Kimo knew she was chanting. Then he saw her raise the bottle and throw it. It crashed against the cooling lava and shattered into pieces that dropped into cracks or melted and were swallowed by tongues of hot lava. Soon he could see no trace remaining to show where it had fallen.

When she returned to the car, Tutu was in a better mood. "Pele likes gin," she said, with a satisfied chuckle.

"Are we going to Pahoa now?" Kimo asked hopefully, as she started the car.

"Why not?" Tutu said amiably. "We'll go see our friends."

They had not gone far when they glimpsed smoking lava through the trees. Around the next curve, Tutu slammed on the brakes. A low finger of lava had crossed the road, and the trees on each side were burning.

"We'll have to go back," Tutu said, and Kimo's heart fell.

15

TUTU BEGAN to turn the old car around. The road was narrow, and she had to see-saw. She got rattled and stepped too hard on the gas when she put the car in reverse.

Kimo, who was looking back for her, yelled, "Not so fast, Tutu!"

But by the time she got her foot on the brake, the back wheels were off the shoulder. "*Auwe!*" she moaned.

Kimo jumped out. It looked bad, but they might be able to get back on the surfaced road. "Take it easy," he told his grandmother.

But she had killed the engine. She tried and tried, but she could not get it started again.

The air was oppressively hot. The broken-crockery noises of cracking lava and the whoosh and crackle of burning trees were all around them. The lava was moving fast, and Kimo saw, with apprchension, that it had taken the easy path and was moving down the surfaced road toward them. The metal of the car began to feel hot, and his lungs smarted from the smoke.

Tutu cried, "*Auwe!* Alas!" and reproached her traitorous friend and called on the Lord. But she could not start the car.

Fluff's cries were shrill with fright. Kimo lifted her box from the back seat. "We can go through the forest, Tutu."

Perspiration had appeared on her broad face. "Sure," she agreed. "It's only an old car." She climbed out, but they lingered to watch, fascinated, as the lava crept closer.

Suddenly there were shouts from across the lava. "Get back! Get away from the car!"

The shouts came from the jeeps that had come down the road on the other side of the lava barrier. Several men jumped out. One of them was Dr. Gerard, who was in the first jeep. He was talking into his radio even while he made gestures waving them back.

Two men from the second jeep dashed into the trees.

"They think it's going to explode!" Kimo yelled. Clutching Fluff's box, he ran back the way they had come, and Tutu followed him, light on her feet in spite of her great weight.

There was a crashing in the trees beside them, and the two men who had forced their way through the forest around the lava burst out on the road. Both had cameras slung from straps around their necks.

"Better hit the ditch, Tutu," one of them called and throwing himself down on his stomach beside the road, he began taking pictures of the car silhouetted against the burning trees behind it.

Kimo was jerked down with Tutu's great body shielding him. A flash of flame enveloped the car, and soon it was burning furiously, a sight to see. The two photographers got up and went closer, snapping pictures.

Tutu got up, dusted off her *muumuu*, and posed for one of them with the burning car in the background.

A few moments later, Kimo heard the sound of a motor behind them and turned to see Big Dan driving up in his patrol car.

"Here you are," he said smiling. "I went by your house for you. Climb in, and I'll take you to Pahoa."

When they were settled in the back seat, he turned the patrol car around and sped back the way they had come. All the way back to the coast, up to the lighthouse point, and in to Pahoa by the lighthouse road, they listened to the reports coming in on Big Dan's radio.

The fourteenth house had burned. The lava was overflowing the dikes built to divert it from the village school. Already half the village was buried beneath the lava, and now it appeared the school was lost. The governor had declared it a disaster area, and there were offers of new land on which the villagers could build new homes. The Hawaiian church was still standing.

Tutu clucked and sighed until the report about the church. Then she gave a satisfied grunt.

When they arrived at Pahoa school gym, Kimo had to give up Fluff's box. The Red Cross lady assigned two cots to them and gave Tutu some blankets.

"They will be serving supper in the cafeteria in a few minutes," she told them. "Why don't you go over there now? There will be plenty of time to make up your beds."

In the cafeteria, they squeezed past a Chinese grandfather eating his rice with chopsticks and joined a long line of evacuées of all ages and sizes waiting to have their plates filled by the volunteer ladies behind the counter.

Tutu called greetings to her many friends ahead of them in the line or already seated at tables. She took the baby from the arms of the tired-looking woman next to her and bounced it gently as she asked about its mother's health.

"Eh, Tutu, you here too?" they called to her from all over the room, and she answered all with her deep chuckle and broad smile.

"*Ae*, all my friends here. Why not me too?"

Everyone was happy to see her.

"Has the church gone yet, Tutu?" they asked her.

"Pele won't take our church," she assured everyone.

Tokiko waved at Kimo from across the room. He gave her a little wave in return, but he was watching for Hiroshi. His friend came in late. Kimo gave him the high sign, and Hiroshi brought his plate and squeezed in on the bench beside Kimo.

"Did you know your grandmother was the last person out?" he whispered.

"Our car caught fire," Kimo whispered back.

Hiroshi ate rapidly, and Kimo found himself trying to keep up with him. "Come on," Hiroshi said, when he had finished.

Tutu made no protest when Kimo got up, for older people were still coming through the line and standing with their plates in their hands looking for a place to sit.

Hiroshi led the way back to the basement office. "This is more fun than watching television in the gym!" he said, as bright-eyed as ever. "But we have to be quiet."

They sidled into the office and squatted down against the wall as before and were soon lost in fascination, as the telephones rang, reports came in, messages were dispatched, and the dark outline of lava grew on the map on the wall.

Miss Prince came in and relieved a man at one of the telephones. She saw them, huddled against the wall, and winked at them. Kimo grinned and ducked his head.

He heard the report come in that the lava had slowed back of the Hawaiian church and it still stood. No one seemed to know just why.

As the evening went on, someone was always asking, "Has the church gone yet?"

The answer was always the same. "The lava is moving around it."

Kimo's heart seemed to swell inside him. Just like Tutu's grandfather's farm! he thought.

It was quite late when Dr. Gerard came in, looking very weary, bringing the news that the houses on Pohai road were burning.

For some reason, Kimo thought first of the knife he had left stuck in the papaya tree in the orchard. He could see them burning together and regretted that he had forgotten to go back for it. Then he realized the knife still would be burning if he had hung it on its hook by the back door. After that he remembered their television set — burning too.

"The lava has come to a stop behind the church," Dr. Gerard was saying. "It was close enough to scorch it slightly, but now it is cooling, and I think the church is safe."

Excitement brought Kimo to his feet. This was the greatest evidence of all!

"Does this mean the eruption may be coming to an end?" one of the men asked the scientist.

"Not necessarily. It means the lava slowed long enough so that it cooled and formed a rock wall, which is now diverting it into a slight depression bypassing the church."

"Curious!"

"How do you explain it?" asked Miss Prince.

Dr. Gerard shrugged. But before he could speak, Kimo cried, "I can explain it!"

Bursting with victory, he ran over to them. "Tutu made Pele an offering, so she would stop being angry. I saw her throw the bottle in the lava right behind the church. That's why Pele spared it, Miss Prince."

Miss Prince had a very odd look on her face. She glanced at Dr. Gerard, then looked at Kimo again.

"Maybe God saved the church," she said gently. "After all, it is His house."

Kimo caught his breath. "That is true. I should have thought of that," he admitted.

"We think it is quite natural for the lava to change direction and follow a slight depression away from the church," Dr. Gerard said quizzically. "And those men who have been out there fighting the lava for three days have the idea that the dikes they threw up helped divert the flow."

"I'm sure they helped," Miss Prince said, flushing a little.

Kimo looked from one to the other, his shoulders sagging. "Then Tutu is wrong?"

Dr. Gerard put a hand on his shoulder. "Don't treat your grandmother's beliefs too lightly," he said. "Perhaps a few hundred years from now scientists will think what I believe to be the truth is as fantastic as the notion that a goddess lives in the firepit seems to me."

The smile on his weary face was warm with understanding.

Kimo looked from him to his teacher. Her smile shed a radiance on him. "All the same," she reminded him gently, "you should never be rude to a strange woman."

Kimo smiled back at them. He had the feeling this was an important moment, one he would remember and think about many times.

"It's time you boys hit the sack, isn't it?"

"Yes, sir," Hiroshi agreed reluctantly, and they left the office.

"He's the best volcanologist in the whole world!" Hiroshi said extravagantly, as they ran toward the gym.

"And Miss Prince is the best teacher!" Kimo exclaimed, not to be outdone.

He ran beside Hiroshi, breathing in gulps of air, which was cleaner and sweeter up here above the volcano, and feeling oddly happy. It seemed strange now that once he had thought of Hiroshi as his worst enemy. He decided that the next time they picked sides for volley ball, he would choose Hiroshi.

The gym was darkened and the chairs empty in front of the blank television screen in the corner. They parted silently.

Tutu was on her cot, but her eyes were open. Whispering, Kimo told her their house was gone, but the church still stood.

Tutu was silent for a long moment. Then she said forgivingly, "Pele meant to spare our house, Kimo. Perhaps it would not have burned if the men had not made their dikes."

Kimo busied himself crawling under his blanket and settling into a comfortable spot.

After a moment, his grandmother added softly, "She is not too angry, or she would have taken everything." And then she began to comfort him, saying, "Don' worry. We'll fin' another house."

Kimo smiled in the darkness, and his heart swelled with love.

Some Definitions and Pronunciations
*(Hawaiian words are marked *; Japanese, †)*

Word	Pronunciation	Definition
*aa	ah-*ah*	lava with a rough clinkery surface
*ae	*ah*-ay	yes
*ai	eye	Oh!
*aia	*eye*-ya	There!
*aloha	a-*lo*-ha	hello, good-bye
*auwe	ow-*way*	alas!
basalt	bay-*salt*	a dark heavy lava, common in Hawaii
crater	*cray*-ter	the bowl-shaped depression at the top of a volcano
caldera	cal-*der*-a	a large depression usually formed by the sinking of part of a mountain top
eruption	e-*rup*-shun	outburst of melted rock from a volcano
geochemist	je-o-*kem*-ist	one who studies the chemical changes in the composition of the earth's crust
graben	*grab*-en	a ditch formed by the sinking of earth between two faults in the earth's crust
*Hanalei	*Ha*-na-lay	Henry
*haole	*how*-lee	white-skinned or foreign person
*haupia	how-*pee*-a	coconut pudding
†hibachi	hi-*bot*-chee	charcoal grill
†Hiroshi	He-*ro*-shee	boy's name
*holua	ho-*lu*-a	sled with a single runner used by native Hawaiians on steep grassy slopes
*Hoopai	*Ho*-pie	proper name
*Kealoha	Kay-a-*lo*-ha	proper name
*keiki	*kay*-kee	child
*Kilauea	Kee-la-*way*-a	Hawaiian volcano
*Kimo	*Kee*-mo	boy's nickname
*Lani	*La*-nee	girl's name

lapilli	la-*pill*-eye	small droplets of lava tossed out by a volcano
lava	*la*-va	hot liquid rock at the earth's surface; also solid products of a volcanic eruption
*lehua	lay-*hu*-a	feathery red blossom of the *ohia* tree
lichee	*lee*-chee	the Chinese *litchi* tree or its fruit, which is eaten fresh or dried
magma	*mag*-ma	hot liquid rock
*mahalo	ma-*ha*-lo	thank you
mango	*mang*-go	large oblong fruit of the tropical mango tree, which tastes something like a peach
*Mookini	Mo-*kee*-nee	proper name
*muumuu	*mu*-mu	Hawaiian dress introduced by the missionaries, usually hanging straight and full from a yoke
mynah	*my*-na	a bird of the starling family introduced from India, very numerous in Hawaii, sometimes caged and taught to speak
*Oana	O-*ah*-na	proper name
*ohelo	*o*-hay-lo	a low-growing Hawaiian shrub with red berries, which in the old days were sacred to Pele
*ohia	*o*-he-a	native Hawaiian tree said to be the first to take root in new lava, whose red blossoms were sacred to Pele
olivine	ol-i-*veen*	a green mineral found in Hawaiian igneous rock, magnesium iron silicate
Pahoa	Pa-*ho*-a	town on the Puna coast of the island of Hawaii

*pahoehoe	*pa*-hoy-hoy	lava with a smooth or ropy surface
papaya	pa-*pie*-ya	yellow, melonlike fruit of the papaya tree
Pele	*Peh*-lee	a lesser Hawaiian goddess said to live in the volcano Kilauea
plumeria	plu-*mer*-ya	a fragrant flower popular for making leis in Hawaii; the famed "frangipani" of India and Ceylon
*Pohai	*Po*-high	circle or group, as of trees; here the name of a street
*Poki	*Po*-kee	often used as a name for a spotted dog
*pupule	pu-*pu*-lee	crazy
seismograph	*size*-mo-graf	an instrument for measuring and recording earthquakes
seismic	*size*-mik	pertaining to, or caused by an earthquake
†teriyaki	ter-ree-*ya*-kee	a barbecue sauce made with soy sauce, garlic, ginger, and sugar
tiltmeter	*tilt*-me-ter	an instrument for measuring slight angles of volcanic tilt, showing swelling and receding of a volcano
†Tokiko	To-*kee*-ko	girl's name
*tutu	*tu*-tu	grandmother, or old woman
volcano	vol-*kay*-no	an opening in the earth's crust through which lava is expelled, gradually forming a cone-shaped mountain with a cup-shaped crater at its top
volcanologist	vol-ca-*nol*-o-jist	one who makes a scientific study of volcanoes
*wahinc	wah-*hee*-nee	woman, wife
†Yamasaki	Ya-ma-*sa*-kee	proper name
†Yuka	*Yu*-ka	girl's name
†zori	*zo*-ree	sandal